"Have you named your dragon yet?" asked Joe.

"Not yet, I'm still thinking," I replied.

MOONLIGHT

MOONLIGHT

Everyone had a name for their dragon. Everyone that is, but me. I wanted his name to be just right though, so I kept thinking.

When I wasn't thinking about names for my dragon, I was thinking about how to win the race.

Joe was the best at everything he did, especially when it came to dragons. His dragon had the perfect name. His dragon was the fastest. His dragon always won.

"Joe might be better, his dragon might be faster, but what if we work harder?" I thought to myself.

So my dragon and I started training.

We got up early to practice our flying.

We ate our special snacks.

And we got lots of dream time.

We were ready, except for that one thing.

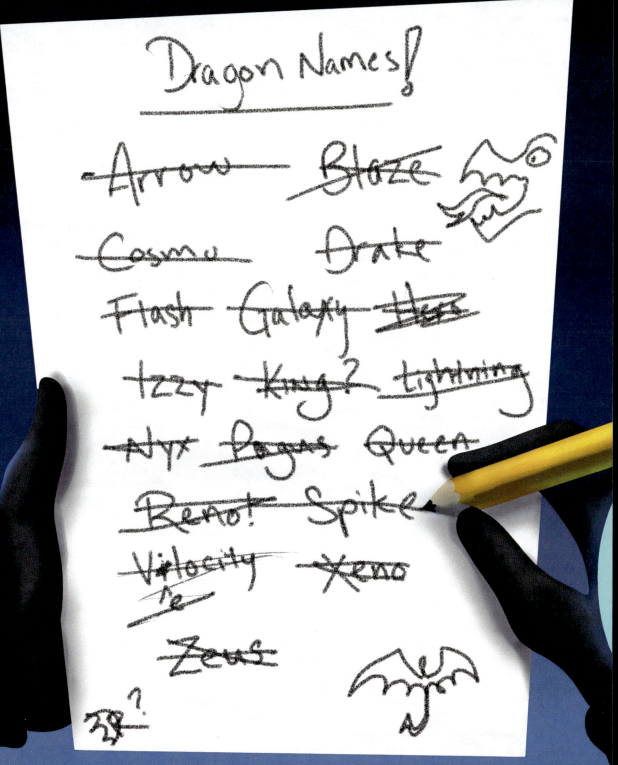

The race was about to start and I still didn't have a name for my dragon. *Can a dragon win if he doesn't have a name?*

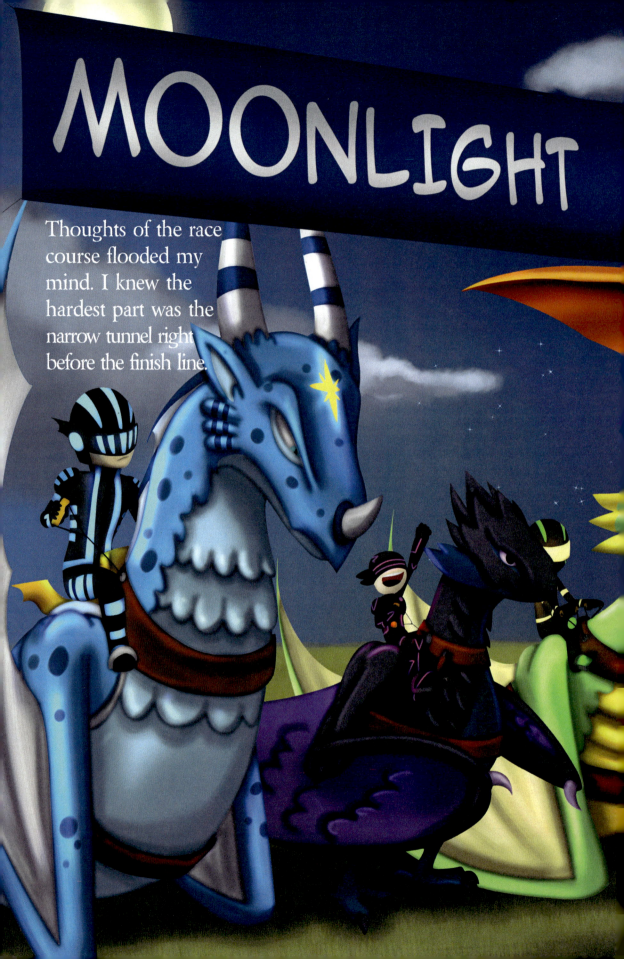

MOONLIGHT

Thoughts of the race course flooded my mind. I knew the hardest part was the narrow tunnel right before the finish line.

There was only room for one dragon at a time. The winds there were strong and could send a dragon into a tail spin if they missed the opening.

We had to get there first!

MARATHON

"Let's go, dragon!" I yelled.
"Or we'll be eating dragon dust again."

MOONLIGHT MARATHON

That woke him up.
He hates dragon dust.

"Come on!" I whispered. "I wish I had named you before the race. Maybe if you had a name you would go faster."

I could hear the crowd going crazy. I felt my dragon speeding up as we passed dragon after dragon.

I could see Joe and Dart were in first place.
Could we catch them?

My heart was pounding. My hands were sweating. My body shivered.

Giant moon shadows danced below us as the wings of my dragon glistened brightly.

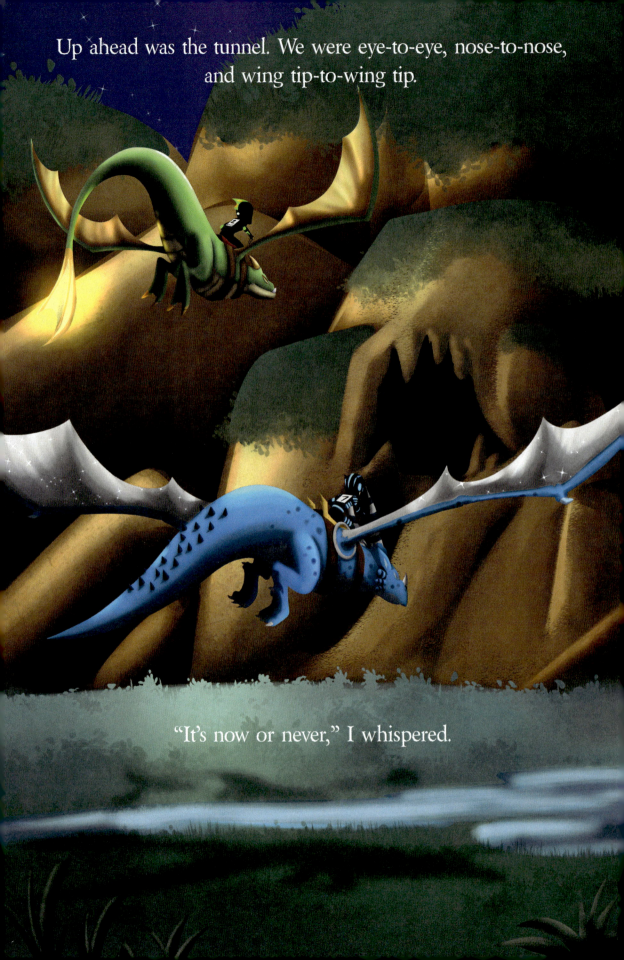

Up ahead was the tunnel. We were eye-to-eye, nose-to-nose, and wing tip-to-wing tip.

"It's now or never," I whispered.

The finish line was right in front of us.

I heard Joe cry out. Joe never asked for help.

HELP!

They were picking up speed as the ground got closer. "Go faster, dragon!" I screamed.

They kept falling…
down,
down,
down.

We weren't going to get there in time. That was my best friend!

Suddenly the light of the moon caught under my dragon's wings and the sky lit up.

"Come on, Moonlight!"

The moment I spoke his name,
I knew something changed.

One minute we were flying through the air on a rescue ride and the next...

"Are you OK, buddy?" I asked. "What just happened?"

"Ummm…I might have forgotten to tell you. When you name your dragon, they get a superpower. Dart is fast for sure, but your dragon can travel at the speed of Moonlight!"

DRAGON NAMES	SUPERPOWERS
Astra	Dream Manipulation
Breeze	Underwater Breathing
Caia	Gravity Control
Drake	Fire Breath
Emerald	Mind Reader
Flash	Super Speed
Galaxy	See the future
Helix	Can heal wounds
Idros	Super Strength
Jinx	Time Freeze
Kismet	Fly in Outer Space
Lynx	Super Hearing
Magog	Time Jumper
Nero	Wish Granter
Onyx	Shadow Smoke
Pippa	Sky Jumper
Qira	X-Ray Vision
Solstice	Turn into Unicorn
Titan	Become Giant Size
Ugo	Ice breath
Varci	Shape Shifter
Warok	Invisibility
Xeno	Super Roar
Yara	Steel Skin
Zap	Lightning Breath

MY DRAGON'S NAME IS: _____

MY DRAGON'S SUPERPOWER IS: _____

This book is dedicated to everyone that believes in dragons!

No creative endeavor is possible without many folks that help along the way and this book is no exception. I would like to thank each and every person that had any part in bringing this story to life.

I would especially like to thank my boyfriend, Brian, for his tireless patience, brilliant ideas and stellar support.

Thank you to my daughter, Calli Rae, for her creative input on the dragon rider costumes.

Thank you to my three children for encouraging me, my grandsons for inspiring me and my mother, Betty Jean, for always believing in me.

I would also like to thank the Butler and Henderson families for allowing their young ones to be part of my books.

Last but not least, I would like to thank my amazing illustrator, Daniel Howard. He never says it can't be done, he just, "makes it so."

Copyright @ 2021 by Cynthia Star.

All rights reserved. This book or any portion thereof may not be reproduced or used in any manner whatsoever without the express written permission of the publisher except for the use of brief quotations in a book review.

Contact: Facebook/Cynthia Star books @cynthiastarbooks

Made in the USA
Las Vegas, NV
26 October 2022